This book belongs to

_____

_____

_____

For Mum
–MC

For Cassie
–VC

tiger tales
an imprint of ME Media, LLC
202 Old Ridgefield Road, Wilton, CT 06897
This paperback edition published 2004
Published in hardcover in the United States 2002
Originally published in Great Britain 2002
By Little Tiger Press
An imprint of Magi Publications
Text copyright ©2002 Michael Catchpool
Illustrations copyright ©2002 Vanessa Cabban
Printed in Belgium

1 3 5 7 9 10 8 6 4 2

Library of Congress Cataloging-in-Publication Data

Catchpool, Michael.
  Where there's a bear, there's trouble! / by Michael Catchpool ;
illustrated by Vanessa Cabban.
     p. cm.
Summary: One bear follows one bee, but instead of honey, he finds trouble.
  ISBN 1-58925-022-2 (hardcover)
  ISBN 1-58925-389-2 (paperback)
  [1. Bears—Fiction. 2. Animal sounds—Fiction. 3. Counting.] I. Cabban,
Vanessa, 1971- ill. II. Title.
  PZ7.C268785 Wh 2002
  [E]—dc21
                              2002002302

Where There's a Bear, There's Trouble!

by Michael Catchpool   Illustrated by Vanessa Cabban

tiger tales

One brown bear saw one yellow bee. And one yellow bee saw one brown bear.

One brown bear thought, "Where there's a bee there's honey . . . sticky honey, yummy honey, drippy honey, gummy honey. I'll follow this bee as quietly as can be."

One yellow bee thought, "Where there's a bear there's trouble. I'll buzz off home as quickly as can be."

So one yellow bee buzzed off over the stone wall . . .

followed by one brown bear,
as quietly as could be on his
softest tip-toes.

Buzz! Buzz! Growl! Growl! Shh!

Two greedy geese spotted one tip-toeing bear. "Ah-ha," they thought. "Where there's a bear there are berries... ripe berries, juicy berries, plump berries, squishy berries. Let's follow that bear as quietly as can be."

So two greedy geese followed
one brown bear, and one brown
bear followed one yellow bee…

Buzz! Buzz! Growl! Growl! Honk! Honk! Shh!

all going along as quietly as can be.

Three shy mice spied two flapping geese.
"Ah-ha," they thought, "where there are
geese, there's corn...

yellow corn, yummy corn, delicious corn, tasty corn. Let's follow those geese as quietly as can be."

Buzz! Buzz! Growl! Growl! Honk! Honk! Squeak.

So one yellow bee buzzed over the bramble bush, and one brown bear followed one yellow bee, and two greedy geese followed one brown bear, and three shy mice followed two greedy geese, all going along as quietly as could be!

Then one yellow bee buzzed right into its nest . . .

Squeak! Shh!

and one hundred yellow
bees buzzed out!

One brown bear saw one hundred yellow bees, and one hundred yellow bees saw one brown bear.

"HELP!" growled one brown bear. "Where there's a swarm there must be

TROUBLE!

I'll run back home as quickly as can be!"

And off he raced, back through the prickly bramble bush.

"Help!" squawked the two greedy geese. "The bear is after us!" And off they flapped across the muddy field.

"Help!" squeaked the three shy mice. "The geese are after us!" And off they scrambled through a crack in the stone wall, until . . .

Growl! Ouch!

Squawk! Hiss!

Squeak! Eek!

BOUNCE . . .

WOBBLE . . .

CRASH!

One yellow bee landed on one brown bear, and one brown bear landed on two greedy geese, and two greedy geese landed on three shy mice.

And one yellow bee thought, "I knew there'd be trouble!"